Caillou®
Sends a Letter

Adaptation of the animated series: Joceline Sanschagrin
Illustrations taken from the animated series and adapted by Eric Sévigny

 chouette COOKIE JAR

Caillou was coloring. His mommy was singing. The sunlight poured into the kitchen. "What a wonderful sunny day!" Mommy exclaimed happily.

"Here's the mail!" said Mommy.

All sorts of colored envelopes fell on top of Gilbert, who was dozing in front of the door. Caillou ran to pick up the mail and handed it to Mommy.

Mommy opened one of the envelopes.
"Bills, nothing but bills.
I'd sure like to get a letter once in a while."

"What's the matter, Caillou?"
Daddy asked.
Caillou explained that Mommy was disappointed with the mail that came every day.
"Mommy would like to get a nice letter," Caillou said.
"Why don't you send a letter to Mommy? Your picture would make a wonderful letter, Caillou!"

"We could send my picture by mail?" Caillou asked.
"Absolutely! And the mailman could deliver it tomorrow morning," Daddy promised.
Caillou thought it was a wonderful idea.
"Now we need an envelope and a stamp," said Daddy.

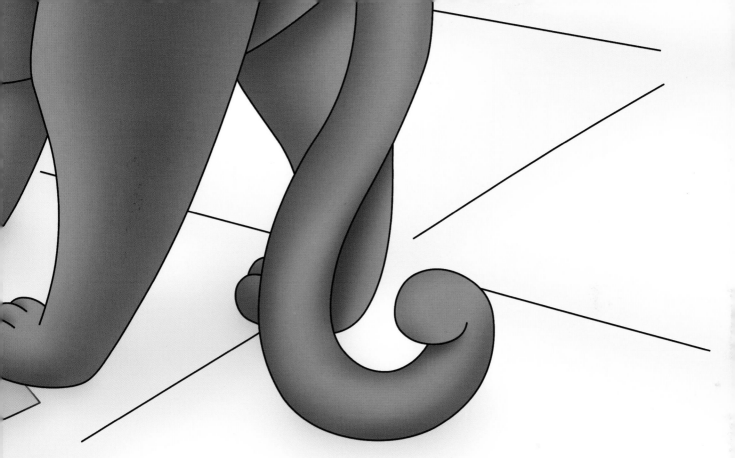

While Caillou was looking for a stamp, Gilbert walked on
the picture lying on the floor. He left a perfectly clear paw
print on it!
"Oh, Gilbert!" Caillou groaned when he saw the paw print.
Caillou heard Mommy coming back.
"Caillou, where are you?" she called.

Caillou quickly hid his paper
under the table.
"What are you two up to?"
Mommy asked.
"Nothing, nothing at all,"
Daddy replied. And he winked
at Caillou.

That night, Caillou got his letter ready.
"Tomorrow we'll have to get up very early," Daddy said as he folded the picture. Then he slipped it into the envelope. After he put the stamp on, Caillou looked at his letter. "Wow!" He thought his letter was perfect. Mommy would be very surprised.

The next morning, Daddy woke Caillou up very early. They tiptoed downstairs and went out to meet the mailman. Caillou gave him the letter.

Caillou called out,
"Mommy, the mailman's
coming! Hurry!"
Mommy arrived just in time
to see all the envelopes
land on the floor.
Caillou could hardly stand
still while Mommy opened
his envelope.
"Oh, Caillou! What a
wonderful surprise! Your
picture is very beautiful.
And you even got Gilbert
to sign it!"

"Thank you very much, Caillou. I'll keep this letter forever,"
Mommy said, giving him a kiss.
"Forever? Wow!" said Caillou.
Mommy was happy. She put Caillou's picture up on
the refrigerator.
"It's the best mail I've ever received!"

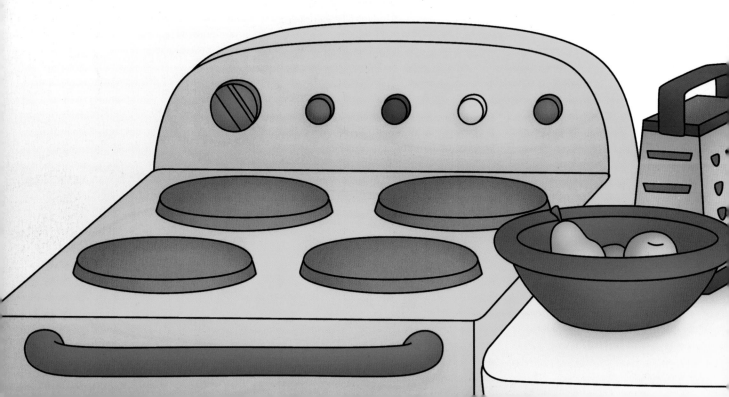

Adaptation of text by Joceline Sanschagrin based on the scenario of the CAILLOU animated
film series produced by Cookie Jar Entertainment Inc. (© 1997 CINAR Productions (2004) Inc.,
a subsidiary of Cookie Jar Entertainment Inc.).
All rights reserved.
Original story written by Christel Kleitch.
Illustrations taken from the television series CAILLOU and adapted by Eric Sévigny.
Art Direction: Monique Dupras

The PBS KIDS logo is a registered mark of PBS and is used with permission.

We acknowledge the financial support of the Government of Canada through
the Canada Book Fund for our publishing activities.

[✦] Canadian   Patrimoine
Heritage   canadien

We acknowledge the support of the Ministry of Culture and Communications
of Quebec and SODEC for the publication and promotion of this book.
SODEC
Québec ❖❖

Bibliothèque et Archives nationales du Québec and Library and Archives
Canada cataloguing in publication

Sanschagrin, Joceline, 1950-
Caillou sends a letter
New ed.
(Clubhouse)
Translation of: Caillou envoie une lettre.
Originally issued in series: Backpack Collection. c1999.
For children aged 3 and up.

ISBN 978-2-89450-866-4

1. Postal service - Juvenile literature. 2. Letter writing - Juvenile literature.
I. Sévigny, Éric. II. Title. III. Series: Clubhouse.

HE6078.S2613 2012   j383   C2011-942123-2

Printed in China
10 9 8 7 6 5 4 3 2 1 CHO1819 JAN2012